A Crow of His Own

Megan Dowd Lambert
Illustrated by David Hyde Costello

SCHOLASTIC INC.

To Rory—M. D. L.

For Ruth Whinnem, a librarian who loved books and
the kids who read them—D. H. C.

ISBN 978-1-338-03007-5

Text copyright © 2015 by Megan Dowd Lambert.
Illustrations copyright © 2015 by David Hyde Costello.
All rights reserved. Published by Scholastic Inc.,
557 Broadway, New York, NY 10012, by arrangement
with Charlesbridge Publishing, Inc. SCHOLASTIC
and associated logos are trademarks and/or registered
trademarks of Scholastic Inc.

The publisher does not have any control over and
does not assume any responsibility for author or
third-party websites or their content.

12 11 10 9 8 7 6 5 4 3 2 1   17 18 19 20 21

Printed in the U.S.A.   40

First Scholastic printing, April 2016

Illustrations done in watercolor on Strathmore paper
Display type set in Fink Roman
Text type set in ITC Goudy Sans
Designed by Susan Mallory Sherman

Author's Note

Clyde's story is about finding a distinctive voice,
so I made the speech and banter of the barnyard
characters sound unique. Rather than using the
dialogue tags "said" or "asked" again and again,
I played around with a variety of verbs. I hope
readers will enjoy discovering the many ways
the characters speak on Sunrise Farm.

When Larry was called off to new opportunities, Sunrise Farm suddenly found itself without its prized rooster. The animals overslept and no one knew what to do.

"Not to worry," soothed Farmer Jay.

"We have a plan," added Farmer Kevin.

Their plan turned out to be a scrawny little guy named Clyde. "Well, he-hello there, neighbors," he stammered. The animals yawned and shuffled their feet.

Roberta was nothing if not a motherly goose. After taking
a gander at Clyde, she took him under her wing.

"Welcome," she chirped. "I'm Roberta."

"Hello," he replied shyly.

"Don't worry about the others. They just miss Larry," she assured him.

"Who's Larry?" inquired Clyde.

The animals' words left Clyde in a state of speechless distress.

"There, there, now, Clyde," Roberta began. "Larry wasn't a genius . . . he just made quite a show of it."

"A show, huh?" Clyde mused. "Thanks, Ruby! You're the best!"

"It's Roberta . . . ," she sighed.

Clyde spent the whole day gathering props, designing his costume, and choreographing a sublime two-step.

He hardly slept a wink that night. Could he do it? Could he live up to Larry's legacy? Could he put on a show of a crow?

After recovering from his initial embarrassment, Clyde hurried past
the disapproving hens and rededicated himself to rehearsing.
"I'll be on my grade-A game tomorrow!" he reassured Roberta.

As the sun peeked over the hillside the next day, a weary Clyde
assumed his position atop the coop, opened his beak, and . . .

. . . promptly fell to the ground with an undignified croak.

"Are you okay?" fussed Roberta.

Clyde was not okay. He was humiliated. He had a crick in his comb, his right wing was all wrong, and his wattle? Well, his wattle was a wobbly wreck.

And yet Clyde was determined to get back in the saddle, so to speak.
"Oh, my!" said Farmer Jay.

Sheriff CLYDE

Roller Skates   For Birds!

"Try, try again," encouraged Farmer Kevin.
Try, try again he would, but . . .

. . . adding a dramatic aerial entrance didn't work out so well the next morning.

As the animals trudged away, disgruntled and dismayed, Roberta stayed behind with Clyde.

"I'll never be a showman like Larry," lamented Clyde.

Even though she was a goose, Roberta clucked with pity.

"Oh, Clyde," she implored. "Forget about Larry. Just crow your own crow."

"Crow my own crow, huh?" he snuffled. "What about the show? No lights, no costumes?"

"Definitely forget about those," Roberta advised.

"Even the mustache?" Clyde asked.

"Save it for special occasions," she answered.

And the next morning . . .

"Enough to give you goose bumps!" exclaimed Roberta.

And with that, Clyde took a deep breath, gave a shake of his comb, and called out another crow of his own.